Jamie SHORT, KING of the COURT

By Katy Duffield
Illustrated by Karl West

rourkeeducationalmedia.com

www.rourkeeducationalmedia.com

Edited by: Keli Sipperley
Cover layout by: Rhea Magaro-Wallace
Interior layout by: Kathy Walsh
Cover and interior illustrations by: Karl West

Library of Congress PCN Data

Jamie Short: King of the Court / Katy Duffield
(Good Sports)
ISBN 978-1-64369-046-9 (hard cover)(alk. paper)
ISBN 978-1-64369-092-6 (soft cover)
ISBN 978-1-64369-193-0 (e-Book)
Library of Congress Control Number: 2018955965

Printed in the United States of America,
North Mankato, Minnesota

Table of Contents

Chapter One

Blobfish Rule!

I'm Jamie Short. I play basketball. Sometimes Coach Goats says I'm too hard on myself. But I can't help it. I LOVE basketball!

"Game time!" I yell to Trini.

Trini holds up a goopy glob of gunk. "I brought Blobbie!"

I poke my finger into the goo. “Go Blobfish!” I yell.

“The Hot Shots play hard,” Coach says. “Go out there and give it your best.”

Principal Ponytail trots onto the court. His tie-dyed tie swings side to side. “Play ball!” he yells.

Chapter Two

Try, Try Again

The referee tosses the ball into the air. A Hot Shots player tips it to his teammate. I stick right with him.

"Good **defense**, Jamie!" Coach yells.

Robby **steals** the ball! He passes it to me. I shoot. A Hot Shots player hits my arm.

The referee blows his whistle.

"Hot Shots foul!" he calls.

I step to the line to shoot **free throws**. I can make these easy-peasy.

But when I shoot the first shot ... CLANG! The ball bounces off the rim.

I shoot the second shot.

CLANG!

"Oh no," I groan. I can't believe I missed both shots.

“Hang in there!” Trini yells as she sprints past.

But I can’t stop thinking about it. I missed. Twice!

The Hot Shots score again and again.

They're good, I think. *And I'm not.*

I play hard. But I keep messing up. I **dribble** the ball off my foot. I throw it **out of bounds.**

I'm no king of the court, I think.

“Shake it off, Jamie!”

Coach calls.

I keep trying.

Trini dribbles down the court. I am wide open! She passes me the ball. I go in for a **lay-up**. A Hot Shots player fouls again.

Chapter Three

Good Luck Blobbie?

"Oh no," I whisper. I do not want to shoot free throws again.

"You can do this," Robby says.

I step up to the foul line. I focus on the basket. I shoot.

CLANG!

My mouth is dry. My hands shake.

Trini yells, “TIME OUT!”

She jogs over. She pats my arm. Then ... *SPLAT!* She plops Blobbie on top of my head!

"Shoot the ball," she says.

I block out the giggles around me. I try to block out the slime that runs down my forehead. But I can't.

There's only one thing to do. I take a deep breath. And I shoot the ball...

SWISH!

“Blobbie’s a good luck charm!” I tell Trini after the game.

She rolls her eyes. “No, he’s not.”

“But Blobbie helped me make my free throw.”

Trini holds up her hand. "No, he didn't. Having a blobfish on your head distracted you. You weren't thinking about the shot. You were thinking about having a blobfish on your head."

I give Trini a high five and a thank-you hug.

Then I give her one more thing...

SPLAT!

Bonus Stuff!

Glossary

defense (DEE-fens): The action of defending against the other team to keep them from scoring.

dribble (DRIB-uhl): To bounce a ball while walking or running.

free throws (free throhz): Free shots given to a player after a foul.

lay-up (lay up): A shot taken close to the basket as the player moves towards the goal.

out of bounds (out of boundz): The area outside the lines of the court.

steals (steelz): When a player on one side takes the ball away from a player on the other side.

Discussion Questions

1. How did Jamie feel when he missed his free throws?
2. Why didn't Jamie want to shoot free throws the second time?
3. Why did Jamie think Blobbie was a good luck charm?

Activity: One-Handed Basketball

Make a one-person basketball game. You can practice your shot anywhere! Ask an adult to help you poke the hole in the cup.

Supplies

- small paper cup
- tape
- piece of string or yarn, about 15 inches (38 centimeters) long
- aluminum foil

Directions

1. Poke a hole in the bottom of the paper cup.
2. Put a small piece of tape around one end of the string.
3. Put the taped end of the string through the hole and tie the string in a knot inside the cup.
4. Wad the aluminum foil into a ball around the other end of the string.
5. Try to swing the aluminum foil ball into the cup basket.

Writing Prompt

Trini is a good friend to Jamie. Write a story about a time that you were a good friend. Or, write a story about when someone was a good friend to you.

About the Author

Katy Duffield is a writer. Basketball is her favorite sport. She doesn't play, but she loves watching college basketball games on TV at her home in Northeast Florida. Katy's favorite team is the Arkansas Razorbacks. Woo Pig Sooie!

About the Illustrator

Karl West lives and works from a studio on the small island of Portland in Dorset, England. His dogs, Ruby and Angel, lie under his desk while he works, snoring away.